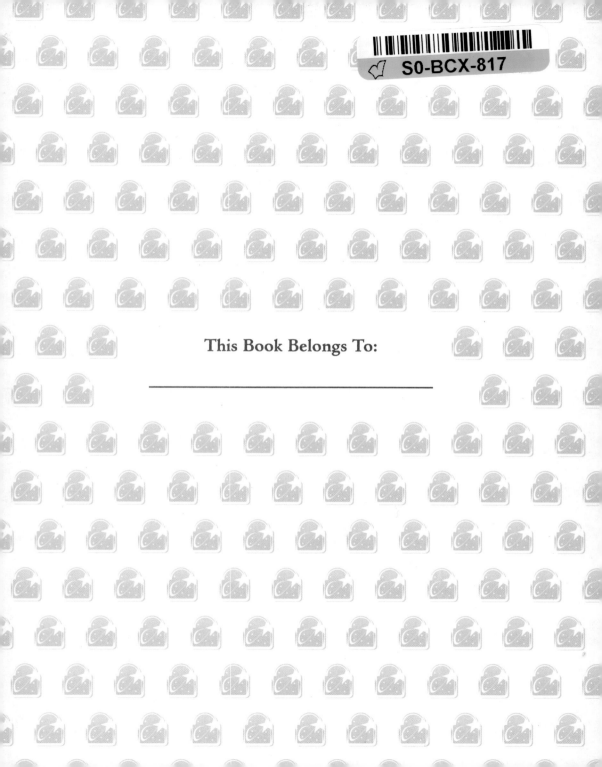

This Book Belongs To:

_____

Other Values To Live By™ Classic Stories

Pinocchio

Wonderful Wizard of Oz

Swiss Family Robinson

Black Beauty

The Jungle Book

www.valuestoliveby.com

ISBN 0-9747133-4-1

"Values to Live By," and the "Values to Live By" logo are Trademarks of Frederic Thomas Inc.
Copyright © 2003 Frederic Thomas Inc., Naples, Florida.
All rights reserved under International and Pan-American Copyright Convention.
No part of this publication may be reproduced, stored in a retrieval system, or transmitted in any form or by any means,
electronic, mechanical, photocopying, recording, or otherwise, without the prior written permission of the copyright owner.
Published in The United States by Frederic Thomas Inc.
Printed in the U.S.A. All rights reserved.
Picture Credits – © Mary Evans Picture Library: Pg. 4 tl, bl; © Sean Sexton Collection/CORBIS: Pg. 4 cr

FREDERIC THOMAS INC.
Produced by: Frederic Thomas Inc., Naples, Florida, Tel: 239-593-8000.

A Classic Story About Responsibility

Treasure Island

By Robert Louis Stevenson

Retold by Kenn Goin

Illustrated by José Miralles

Managing Art Editor Tom Gawle

Senior Editors Elizabeth Jones, Mary Weber

Production Artist Tim Carls

FREDERIC THOMAS INC.

Stevenson's Treasure Island

Where authors get their ideas is a particularly interesting thought for admirers of Treasure Island. It all began in the summer of 1881. The author and his family were on vacation in Scotland. Unfortunately, the weather was particularly cold and rainy, so the travelers spent most of their time indoors.

One day, the author and his twelve-year-old stepson were looking for ways to pass the time. They decided to draw a map of a make-believe island where treasure was buried. They named places on the island, colored the map and eventually moved on to other activities. But the idea of a treasure map stayed with the author and "On a chill September morning, by the cheek of a brisk fire," he wrote, "*Treasure Island* was born."

The book, published in 1883, was an instant and huge success. It made Stevenson, for the first time, a popular and profitable writer. Interestingly, it was his first long piece of narrative fiction and his first writing for children.

Robert Louis Balfour Stevenson was born in Edinburgh, Scotland, on November 13, 1850. He briefly trained as an engineer at Edinburgh University, but then decided to become a lawyer.

Princes Street in Edinburgh, Scotland, circa 1890.

By the time he had his law degree, however, he'd decided to become a writer. From his first book in 1878, it only took him five years to find real success as an author. He traveled widely throughout his life–embracing many of the very swashbuckling ideals incorporated into *Treasure Island*, *Kidnapped*, and other works. When he died in December of 1894, he was buried on a mountain above his home in Samoa.

Robert Louis Stevenson's home at Vailima, Samoa, with Vaea Mountain in the background.

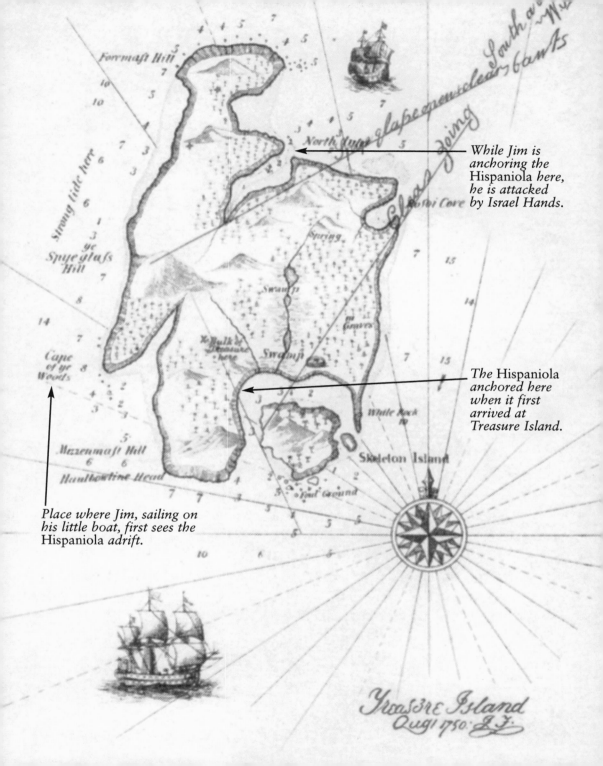

While Jim is anchoring the Hispaniola *here*, he is attacked by Israel Hands.

The Hispaniola anchored here when it first arrived at Treasure Island.

Place where Jim, sailing on his little boat, first sees the Hispaniola *adrift*.

Foremast Hill

Strong tide here

ye Spyeglass Hill

Cape of ye Woods

Mizzenmast Hill

Hauleboline Head

North Inlet

Spring

Swamp

ye Bulk of Treasure here

Swamp

Graves

Swamp

White Rock

Skeleton Island

Foul Ground

Treasure Island
Augt 1750

·⁓ At the Admiral Benbow Inn ⁓·

Squire Trelawney, Dr. Livesay and the rest of these gentlemen having asked me to write down the whole particulars about Treasure Island, from the beginning to the end, keeping nothing back but the bearings of the island, and that only because there is still treasure not yet lifted, I, Jim Hawkins, take up my pen in the year of grace 17— and go back to the time when my father kept the *Admiral Benbow* inn, and the brown old seaman called captain, with the sabre cut, first took up his lodging under our roof.

I remember him as if it were yesterday, as he came plodding to the inn door, his sea-chest following behind him in a hand-barrow. He was a tall, strong, heavy, nut-brown man; his tarry pigtail falling over the shoulders of his soiled blue coat; and the sabre cut across one cheek a dirty, livid white. He was a very silent man by custom but was in the habit of breaking out in that old sea-song:

"Fifteen men on the dead man's chest –
Yo-ho-ho, and a bottle of rum!"

He had taken me aside one day and promised me a silver four-penny on the first of every month if I would only keep my "weather-eye open for a seafaring man with one leg" and let him know the moment he appeared.

It was a January morning, a few months after the captain joined us. He had risen earlier than usual and set out down the beach.

I was laying the breakfast-table when the parlour door opened, and a man stepped in on whom I had never set eyes. He was a pale, tallowy creature.

"Is this here table for my mate, Bill?" he asked, pointing, with a kind of leer.

I told him I did not know his mate Bill. This table was for a person who stayed in our house, whom we called captain.

"Well," said he, "my mate Bill would be called captain. He has a cut on one cheek."

At that moment the captain strode in, slammed the door behind him and marched straight across the room to where his breakfast awaited.

"Bill," said the stranger.

The captain spun around on his heel; all the brown had gone out of his face. I felt sorry to see him, all in a moment, turn so old and sick.

"Black Dog!" the captain said with a gasp.

All of a sudden there was a tremendous explosion of oaths and other noises – the chair and table went over in a lump, then a cry of pain, and the next instant I saw Black Dog in full flight, and the captain hotly pursuing. Black Dog, in spite of his wound, disappeared over the edge of the hill in half a minute.

"Rum!" the captain cried, as he returned and sank into a chair. While fetching the drink, I heard a loud fall in the parlor and, running in, beheld the captain lying on the floor. It was a happy relief when Dr. Livesey, who had come to see my sick father, arrived moments later.

"Oh, doctor," I cried, "Where is he wounded?"

"No more wounded than you or I," said the doctor. "The man has had a stroke from years of drinking rum."

As soon as the doctor revived him, he took me aside and whispered, "I have drawn blood enough to keep him quite a while. He should lie for a week where he is; but another stroke would settle him." ✳

·⁓ The Black Spot ⁓·

Over the next several days, the captain worried aloud about a "black spot," until I finally asked him what the spot was.

"That's a summons, mate. If they come again and I can't get away, mind you it's the oilskin packet in my old sea-chest they're after, you get on a horse and go to Doctor Livesey and tell him to send help. Tell him that Flint's crew are at the *Admiral Benbow*. I was old Flint's first mate, you see. He gave the chest to me at Savannah when he lay a-dying."

A few weeks hence, about three o-clock one bitter, frosty afternoon, I saw someone drawing slowly near along the road. He was plainly blind, for he tapped before him with a stick, and he was hunched, as with age or weakness. He stopped a little from the inn and raised his voice in an odd sing-song:

"Will any kind friend inform a poor blind man, where or in what part of the country he may now be?"

"You are at the *Admiral Benbow*, Black Hill Cove, my good man," said I.

"Will you give me your hand, my kind young friend, and lead me in?" said he.

I held out my hand, and the horrible, soft-spoken, eyeless creature gripped it in a moment like a vice.

"Now boy," he said, "take me in to the captain." I protested but he assured me that he would break my arm if I did not help him. "Lead me straight to him and when I'm in view, cry out, 'Here's a friend for you, Bill.'"

I was so utterly terrified of the blind beggar that as I opened the parlor door I cried out the words he had ordered in a trembling voice.

"Now, Bill, sit where you are," said the beggar. "If I can't see, I can still hear. Hold out your left hand. Boy, take his left hand by the wrist, and bring it near to my right."

We both obeyed him to the letter, and I saw him pass something from the hollow of the hand into the palm of the captain's, which closed upon it instantly.

"And now that's done." Then with amazing accuracy and nimbleness, he skipped out of the parlor and into the road.

The captain looked into his palm. "Ten o'clock!" he cried. "Six hours. We'll do them yet!" and he sprang to his feet.

Even as he did so, he reeled, put his hand to his throat, stood swaying for a moment, and then, with a peculiar sound, fell from his whole height face foremost to the floor. The captain had been struck dead by a thundering stroke.

On the floor, close to the captain's hand, there was a little round of paper, blackened on one side. I could not doubt that this was the black

spot; and taking it up, I found written on the other side, this short message: "You have till ten tonight." Thank goodness, time was on my side. I soon found the key to the chest on a piece of tarry string round the captain's neck.

I was going through the chest's contents when I heard a sound that brought my heart into my mouth – the tap-tapping of the blind man's stick upon the frozen road. Then, I heard a little low whistle sound, a signal, a good way off upon the hill. I quickly took enough money to cover the captain's lodging and retrieved an oilskin packet from the bottom of the trunk before traveling to Dr. Livesey's. ✸

⌁ To Bristol! ⌁

I was shown into Dr. Livesey's library, where he and Squire Trelawney sat on either side of a bright fire.

After I described my circumstance, Dr. Livesey said, "Do you have the thing they were after?"

"Here it is," said I, and gave him the oilskin packet. We found that it contained a book with a list of ships and towns that Flint and his men had sunk or plundered for gold and silver, over nearly 20 years. The packet also held a sealed paper. When the doctor opened it, a map of an island – marked to be nine miles long and five across – fell out. The island had two fine, land-locked harbors and a hill in the center part marked "The Spy-glass." Three crosses of red ink – two on the north part of the island, one in the south-west – were marked along with these words: "Bulk of treasure here."

"Livesey," said the squire excitedly, "tomorrow I start for Bristol. In three weeks' time, we'll have a ship and the choicest crew in England. Hawkins shall come as cabin boy. You, Livesey, are the ship's doctor; I am the admiral."

"We are not the only men who know of this paper," warned Livesey. "Those questionable fellows who visited the *Admiral Benbow*, and more, I dare say, are bound that they'll get that treasure, too. We must exercise care until we get to sea."

* * *

It was a little longer than the squire imagined before we heard from him that we were ready for the sea. But one fine day, the following letter arrived:

Old Anchor Inn, Bristol, March 1, 17—.

Dear Livesey, The ship is bought and fitted. You've never imagined a sweeter schooner, 200 tons, named Hispaniola. *I had the worry of the deuce itself to find so much as half a dozen men, however, till the most remarkable stroke of fortune brought me the very man I required.*

He was an old sailor who wanted a good berth as cook to get to sea again. I engaged him on the spot to be ship's cook. Long John Silver, he is called, and has lost a leg. Well, sir, I thought I had only found a cook, but it was a crew I had discovered. Between Silver and myself we got together in a few days a company of the toughest old salts imaginable.

You and young Hawkins must both come full speed to Bristol.

John Trelawney

When we arrived in Bristol, the doctor and I walked along the quays and beside the great multitude of ships of all sizes and rigs and nations. I saw many old sailors, with rings in their ears and whiskers curled in ringlets, and tarry pigtails, and their swaggering, clumsy sea-walk; and if I had seen as many kings or archbishops I could not have been more delighted.

While I was still in this delightful dream, we came suddenly in front of a large inn, where we met Squire Trelawney, dressed like a sea-officer in stout blue cloth, coming out of the door with a smile on his face and a capital imitation of a sailor's walk.

"Here you all are," he cried. "We sail tomorrow!" ❈

·⁓ Rumors of Mutiny! ⁓·

Within a day, we had boarded our ship and met the crew, including Captain Smollett, Long John Silver, our cook – who came aboard with a parrot perched on his shoulder, and the men. Captain Smollett, when he was alone with us, immediately expressed fears about the crew. It seems that he had learned, through rumors, that this was to be a treasure voyage – a fact we had kept from all but our inner circle. And the crew even knew about the map with the red crosses. The captain suspected treachery. We assured him that we would be on watch.

I am not going to relate the voyage to the Isle of Treasure in detail. It was fairly prosperous. The ship proved to be a good ship, the crew were capable seamen, but before we came to Treasure Island, something happened which requires to be known.

Just after sundown one day, when all my work was over, it occurred to me that I should like an apple. I got bodily into the apple barrel, and found scarce an apple left. But sitting down there in the dark, with the rocking movement of the ship, I either fell asleep, or was on the point of doing so, when a heavy man sat down with a crash close by.

I then heard him speak. It was Silver's voice. Before I had heard a dozen words, I would not have shown myself for all the world. I understood that the lives of all the honest men aboard depended upon me alone.

"The mutiny begins the last moment I can manage," said Silver. "The squire and doctor shall find the treasure, and help us to get it aboard! Then we'll see."

"What do we to do with 'em, then?" asked the seaman.

"I give my vote – death," said Silver.

Just then a sort of brightness fell upon me in the barrel and, looking up, I found the moon had risen. Almost at the same time the voice of the look-out shouted, "Land-ho!" The hills of Treasure Island had been spotted. And the great rush of feet across the deck allowed me to slip outside my barrel, unseen.

Captain Smollett, the squire and Dr. Livesey were talking together on the quarter-deck. Dr. Livesey called for me, which gave me the opportunity to speak: "Doctor. Get the captain and squire down to the cabin and then make some pretense to send for me. I have terrible news," I whispered.

"Thank you, Jim," said he, quite loudly, "that was all I wanted to know," as if he had asked me a question. And with that he turned on his heel and rejoined the other two.

A little while later, I stood before the doctor, squire and captain in one of the cabins.

"Now, Hawkins," said the squire, "speak up."

I did as I was bid, and told the whole details of Silver's conversation. After I spoke, there was much debate about what to do. Because we were unsure of how many men were part of Silver's gang, however, we decided to wait and watch.

"Jim here," said the doctor, "can help us more than any one. The men are not shy with him, and Jim is a noticing lad."

By an odd train of circumstances, it was indeed through me that safety came. ✺

·⁓ About Ben Gunn ⁓·

The inlet in which we anchored the ship was mostly landlocked and buried in woods, the trees coming right down to the high-water mark, the shores mostly flat and the hilltops standing round at a distance. From the ship, we could see nothing of the block-house or stockade noted on the map, for they were quite buried among trees.

There was not a breath of air moving on this gloomy afternoon. The conduct of the men increasingly became threatening. Mutiny, it was plain, hung over us like a thunder-cloud.

To lessen the tension, the captain allowed the men an afternoon ashore. Six fellows were to stay on board, and the remaining 13, including Silver, were to embark in small boats, called gigs, that had been put in the water.

It occurred to me at once to go ashore. In a jiffy, I had slipped over the *Hispaniola's* side and curled up in the bow of the nearest boat. Almost at the same moment, she shoved off.

Our boat reached the beach ahead of the others and the bow neared the shore-side trees. I caught a branch, swung myself out and ran straight before my nose till I could run no longer. I was so pleased at having given the slip to the others, that I began to enjoy myself and look around the strange land that we'd found. Eventually, I came to a long thicket of trees, which grew along the sand like brambles, the boughs curiously twisted.

All at once there began a sort of bustle among the bulrushes as a great cloud of wild ducks flew screaming and circling in the air. I judged at once that my shipmates must be near.

I recognized Silver's voice. Foolhardy as it was, I decided to try to overhear him and the other crewman at their councils. But they had only spoken a few moments when, far away out in the marsh, there arose one horrid, long drawn scream. And when the man Silver had been talking with tried to run away, for he refused to join in the mutiny, Silver struck him with his crutch right between the shoulders in the middle of his back and then leapt upon him with a knife. The killing had begun. The mutineers were attacking the men who would not join in their plot.

Instantly, I began to extricate myself and crawl back again to the more open portion of the wood. As soon as I was clear of the thicket, I ran as I never ran before.

I soon had drawn near to the foot of the little hill with the two peaks and had got into a part of the island where the trees grew more widely apart. Suddenly, I saw a figure leap with great rapidity behind the trunk of a pine. What it was, I could in no wise tell. It seemed dark and shaggy; more I knew not.

"Who are you?" I called.

"Ben Gunn," came the answer. "I haven't spoke with a Christian these three years."

I could now see that he was an Englishman like myself.

His skin was burnt by the sun and his fair eyes looked quite startling in so dark a face.

"Were you shipwrecked?" I asked.

"Nay," said he, "marooned for three years." Then he asked, "What do you call yourself, mate?"

"Jim Hawkins," I told him.

"Well Jim," he said, looking all round him and lowering his voice to a whisper, "I'm rich. And I'll tell you what: I'll make a man of you, Jim." Then he paused, before asking: "It ain't Flint's ship you came here on, is it?"

I explained that Flint was dead, but that some of his crew served aboard the *Hispaniola*.

"Not a man with one leg," he gasped.

"Silver?" I asked.

"Ah, Silver!" says he; "that were his name."

I immediately told him the whole story of our voyage, and the predicament in which we found ourselves.

For his history, Ben Gunn said that he had been on another ship, three years back, when they sighted the island. He knew Flint had buried treasure here, so he persisted until his captain let the men come ashore. Twelve days later, with no treasure found, his mates gave him a musket, spade and pickaxe and said he could find Flint's money on his own.

When Gunn begged me to return to our ship and tell the captain that he would gladly pay a thousand pounds to be allowed passage to return to England, I asked how he thought I would be able to get on board the *Hispaniola* again.

"Ah!" said he, "Well, there's my boat, that I made with my two hands and keep under the white rock. We might try that after dark. Hi!" he broke out, "What's that?"

"They have begun to fight," I cried. "Follow me."

We ran amid the cannon-shots. Then there was a pause. Not a quarter mile in front of me, I beheld the Union Jack flutter in the air above a wood. While I had been on the island, I was to learn, my crew had made camp in the old block-house, part of the stockade still standing at the south end of the island, and the captain had run up the colors from a tree that hung over its roof. ✺

∽ The Battle ∽

As soon as Ben Gunn saw the colors, he came to a halt.
"There are your friends," he said.

"Far more likely mutineers," I answered.

"No!" he cried. "Silver would fly the Jolly Roger. That's your friends. There's been blows, too, and I reckon your friends has had the best of it and here they are ashore in the old stockade."

Before he would let me go, Ben asked that I set up a meeting between himself and the doctor or squire, which I promised to do. I then made my way round the island. The sun had just set and the sea breeze was rustling and tumbling in the woods. The *Hispaniola* still lay where she had anchored and, sure enough, there was the Jolly Roger – the black flag of piracy – flying from her peak.

As I began to make my way toward the stockade, I saw, at some distance away, an isolated rock, pretty high, and peculiarly white in color. It occurred to me that this might be Ben Gunn's white rock, and that some day or other a boat might be wanted, and I should know where to look for one.

At last, I arrived at the block-house and was warmly welcomed by the faithful party. I soon told my story and began to look about me. The log-house was made of unsquared trunks of pine – roof, walls and floor. There was a porch at the door, and under this porch a little spring welled up into an artificial basin of a rather odd kind – no other than a great ship's kettle of iron with the bottom knocked out.

The cold evening breeze whistled through every chink of the rude building and sprinkled the floor with a continual rain of fine sand. Our chimney was a square hole in the roof. Most of the smoke eddied about the house, however, and kept us coughing and wiping the eye.

I was dead tired by this point, as you may fancy. When I got to sleep, after a great deal of tossing, I slept like a log of wood until I was wakened by a bustle and the sound of voices.

"Flag of truce!" I heard someone say. Then, immediately after, with a cry of surprise, "Silver himself!"

"What do you want with your flag of truce?" the captain cried.

"We want that treasure," said Silver. "You give us the treasure map to

get the treasure by, and stop shooting poor seamen, and we'll offer you a choice. Either you come aboard with us, once we have the treasure, and then I'll give you my affy-davy to clap you somewhere safe ashore. Or you can stay here and we'll divide the stores man for man."

"Your affidavit – your word of honor? Is that all?" asked the captain.

"Every last word, by thunder!" answered John.

"Good," said the captain. "Now you'll hear me. If you'll come up one by one, unarmed, I'll engage to clap you all in irons and take you home to a fair trial in England. If you won't, I'll see you all to Davy Jones."

Silver's eyes stared in his head with wrath. He spat into the spring and said, "That's what I think of ye." Then he stumbled off and disappeared among the trees.

Within the hour, the mutineers attacked from all sides. After a fierce battle in which the captain was badly wounded, they at last retreated.

"Five of them will never run again," the doctor said.

"Five," cried the captain. "That leaves us four to eight. That's better odds than we had at starting, when we were seven to 19."

There was no return of the mutineers. They had "got their rations for that day" as the captain put it, and we had the place to ourselves. Shortly after noon, the doctor set off to see Ben Gunn. ✳

·⁓ The Escapade ⁓·

With the others occupied, I decided to slip away and find the white rock I had observed last evening. I was a fool, if you like, and certainly I was going to do a foolish, overbold act, but I was determined to do it. Was it there or not that Ben Gunn had hidden his boat?

I made for the east coast of the island and eventually worked my way down along the beach. I spotted the *Hispaniola* at about the same time that the sun had gone down behind the Spy-glass and the fog was rapidly collecting. The white rock, visible enough above the brush, was still some eighth of a mile further away. As it began to grow dark in earnest, I reached the rock and found the boat – homemade if ever anything was homemade.

Now I had taken a new notion. This was to slip out under cover of the night, cut the pirated *Hispaniola* adrift, and let her go ashore where she fancied. I had quite made up my mind that the mutineers, after their repulse of the morning, had nothing nearer their hearts than to up anchor and away to sea; this I thought, would be a fine thing to prevent.

I waded a little way into the water, and set my boat down on the surface. When I reached the *Hispaniola* and cut the anchor cable, the adrift schooner gave a violent yaw. One shout followed another from on board. Drawn along in the powerful wake of the *Hispaniola*, my little boat became captive to its drift. We went spinning through the inlet narrows for open sea.

I crouched down in the bottom of Gunn's skiff and devoutly recommended my spirit to its Maker. So I must have lain for hours, now and again wetted with flying sprays, until sleep at last supervened and I dreamed of the old *Admiral Benbow*.

It was broad day when I awoke and found myself tossing at the southwest end of Treasure Island. The sun was up but was still hidden from me behind the great bulk of the Spy-glass, which on this side descended almost to the sea – fringed with great masses of fallen rock. I was scarce a quarter of a mile out to sea and it was my first thought to paddle in and land. But I soon gave up that idea when I saw how the breakers spouted among the fallen rocks. If I ventured nearer, I'd be dashed to death.

I decided to leave this shore behind me and try for land at the kindlier-looking Cape of the Woods. Unfortunately, the current carried me past my destination. I soon beheld a sight that changed the nature of my thoughts.

Right in front of me, not half a mile away, I beheld the *Hispaniola* under sail. After watching her erratic movements for a time, I realized that nobody was steering. If so, where were the men? Either they were dead drunk or had deserted her. Perhaps if I could get on board, I might return the vessel to her captain.

At last, I had my chance: I was on the summit of one swell when the schooner suddenly came stooping over the next. The bowsprit was over my head. I sprang to my feet, and leaped. With one hand I caught the jib-boom, while my foot was lodged between the stay and the brace. As I still clung there panting, a dull blow told me that the schooner had charged down upon and struck my little boat, and that I was left without retreat on the *Hispaniola*. ✳

·~ Pieces of Eight! ~·

I crawled along the bowsprit of the *Hispaniola* and tumbled head foremost on the deck.

I discovered only one live pirate on the ship: a wounded Israel Hands, propped against the bulwarks, his face white under its tan.

"Well, Mr. Hands," said I as I drew down the Jolly Roger and chucked it overboard, "I've come aboard to take possession of this ship."

"I reckon," he said, "unless I gives you a hint, you ain't the man to sail this ship. I'll tell you how to sail her if you gives me food and drink and an old scarf to tie my wound up."

Well, there was sense in this. We struck our bargain on the spot, and I provided the requested goods.

After a time, the ship running smoothly, Mr. Hands said, "Shiver my timbers! Can you just get me a bottle of wine, Jim – this here brandy's too strong for my head."

I entirely disbelieved that Hands preferred wine to brandy. The whole story was a pretext. But I saw some value in playing along.

"Some wine?" I said as I scuttled away with all the noise I could, then slipped off my shoes and quietly took a vantage point from which to watch Hands. In half a minute he had picked from a coil of rope a long knife discolored to the hilt with blood and concealed it in his jacket.

I soon reappeared on deck with the wine and while I guided the schooner into North Inlet, Hands drank and issued his commands – "steady," "starboard," "larboard a little." In the excitement of these maneuvers, I let down my guard. When I looked round, there was Hands, already half-way towards me, with the knife in his right hand.

While things stood thus, suddenly the *Hispaniola* struck ground and canted over till the deck stood

at an angle of 45 degrees. Quick as thought, I climbed the mizzen shrouds and did not draw breath till I was seated on the cross-trees of the mast.

Hands hauled himself heavily into the shrouds and, with the knife in his teeth, began slowly and painfully to mount. I warned him that I had a pistol in each hand. All in a breath, he threw the knife, and I was pinned by the shoulder to the mast. In the horrid pain and surprise of the moment, both my pistols went off. Hands plunged headfirst into the water.

The knife had come the nearest in the world to missing me altogether. It held me by a mere pinch of skin and easily came loose.

I lowered myself to the deck and then went below and did what I could for my wound. The ship was now mine. I secured her in the anchorage just as the last rays of sunlight illumined the water, then set out for the block-house and my companions.

When I reached the house, I got on my hands and knees and crawled, without a sound, towards a corner. As I drew nearer, my heart was suddenly lightened. It is not a pleasant noise in itself, but just then it was like music to hear my friends snoring together so loud in their sleep.

All of a sudden, a shrill voice broke forth out of the darkness:

"*Pieces of eight*! *Pieces of eight*! *Pieces of eight*! *Pieces of eight*! *Pieces of eight*!"

and so forth, without pause or change. It was Silver's parrot, Captain Flint! She was keeping better watch than any human being, announcing my arrival with her wearisome refrain. ✺

⤙ A Doctor's Visit ⤙

The red glare of the torch, lighting up the interior of the block-house, showed me the worst of my apprehensions realized. The pirates were in possession of the house and stores. There were six of the buccaneers, all told; not another man left alive.

"So," said Silver, Captain Flint on his shoulder, "here's Jim Hawkins, shiver my timbers!" He warmly welcomed me and suggested that I would have to join his crew now. The captain and doctor, claimed he, were so angry over my slipping away that they would never take me back.

"There's a thing or two I have to tell you," I said, "and the first is this: here you are, in a bad way: ship lost, treasure lost, men lost; your whole business gone to wreck; and if you want to know who did it – it was I!" I then explained the particulars and ended by saying: "Kill me, if you please. But if you spare me, when you fellows are in court for piracy, I'll be a witness to save you from the gallows."

My revelations were more than the men could bear. But above everyone, they blamed Silver for their losses. After angry words, they stormed out of the block-house to hold a council.

"As for that lot and their council," Silver said, "they're outright fools and cowards. Don't worry. I'll save your life from them. But see here, Jim – tit for tat – you save Long John from swinging."

"What I can do, that I'll do," I said.

The council of the buccaneers had lasted some time. Then they re-entered the house – with a black spot for Silver. It seemed Long John was about to be overthrown when, at the last moment, he cast down upon the floor a paper that I instantly recognized – none other than Flint's treasure map with the three red crosses. All at once, all was forgiven. The pirates leaped upon it like cats upon a mouse.

* * *

The next morning, I was delighted when the doctor had come to minister to the wounded among Silver's crew. And Long John took great joy in telling Livesey about my arrival.

As Silver walked with us away from the block-house, so that the doctor and I could talk privately, he said: "Doctor, I'm no coward, but I've the shakes upon me for the gallows. You'll not forget what I done good, I know. And I step aside – see here – and leave you and Jim alone. And you'll put that down for me, too, won't you?"

So saying, he stepped back a little way, till he was out of earshot. There he sat down upon a tree-stump and began to whistle.

The doctor began by gently scolding me for leaving and telling no one. But when he saw my predicament with the pirates, and when I said that what I feared most from them was torture, he encouraged me to make a run for it with him.

"No," I replied, "I gave Silver my word that I would return if he allowed me to speak with you. But know this: I fear torture because I might let slip a word of where the ship is; for I got the ship, part by luck and part by risking."

The doctor was heartened to hear of the ship. "There is a kind of fate in this," he observed. "Every step, it's you that saves our lives; you found out the plot, you found Ben Gunn, and now the ship." And, before leaving, he assured me that my friends would let nothing happen to me at the hands of the pirates. ✷

⟡ Escape from Treasure Island! ⟡

After the doctor left, Silver and I had breakfast with the others and packed for treasure-hunting. Still a mystery to me was my friends' desertion of the stockade and their release of Flint's map to Silver. A few hours later, we reached the slopes of the Spy-glass where our party spread itself out in a fan shape. Suddenly, the man on the farthest left began to cry in terror. When we ran to see what was wrong, we found a human skeleton at the foot of a big pine.

The body was not in a natural position. The man lay perfectly straight – his feet pointing in one direction, his hands, raised above his head like a diver's, pointing directly in the opposite. The men feared the skeleton's position was the work of something unnatural. Silver realized the skeleton had been arranged like a compass.

"I thought so," cried the cook; "this here is a p'inter. And it's one of Flint's jokes. Him and these six was alone here; he killed 'em, every man; and this one he hauled here and laid down by compass! By Thunder! If it don't make me cold inside to think of Flint."

"If ever a sperrit walked, it would be Flint's," said one of the mutineers.

"Ay, that he be," observed another; "how he raged and how he sang. 'Fifteen Men' were his only song, mates; and I tell you true, I never rightly liked to hear it since."

From then on, the terror of the dead buccaneer fell on the mutineers' spirits. They had started speaking lower and lower, so that their talk hardly interrupted the silence of the wood. All of a sudden, a thin, high, trembling voice struck up:

"Fifteen men on the dead man's chest—
Yo-ho-ho, and a bottle of rum!"

I have never seen men more dreadfully affected than the pirates. The color went from their six faces like enchantment. But by the time we had reached the tall trees noted on the treasure chart, the thought of the money had swallowed up their terrors.

Suddenly, a low cry arose from some of the men. When Silver and I got to them, we saw the hole where the treasure had been: the seven hundred thousand pounds were gone!

There never was such an overturn in this world. The buccaneers began to leap, one after another into the pit, and to dig with their fingers.

One of them cried, "Mates. I tell you, now, that Silver there knew it all along. Look in the face of him, and you'll see it wrote there."

They were all set to come at us when three musket-shots flashed out of the thicket. The mutineers ran for their lives. At the same moment the doctor and Ben Gunn joined us, with smoking muskets, from among the trees.

As we followed them down hill, the doctor related that the voice we'd heard earlier had been Ben, preying on the pirate's fears. And Ben, it seems, had found the treasure in his wanderings about the island months ago. He had carried it on his back, in many weary journeys, to a cave.

Knowing this, the doctor had gone to Silver and bargained the unneeded map for their release from the smokey stockade. They then moved to the hill with two peaks to keep a guard upon the money.

The next morning, we began to move the treasure from the cave to the *Hispaniola*. English, French, Spanish, Portuguese, Georges and Louises, doubloons and double guineas and moidores and sequins, the pictures of all the kings of Europe for the last hundred years, strange Oriental pieces stamped with what looked like wisps of string or bits of spider's web, round pieces and square pieces, and pieces bored through the middle, as if to wear them round your neck – nearly every variety of money in the world must, I think, have found a place in that collection.

It took several days to load all the treasure on the *Hispaniola*. Then, early one morning thereafter, we weighed anchor. Before noon, the highest rock of Treasure Island had sunk into the blue round of sea.

It was just at sundown when we cast anchor in a most beautiful, land-locked gulf and were immediately surrounded by boats full of natives. Doctor Livesey and Squire Trelawney, taking me along with them, went ashore to pass the night.

Day was breaking when we returned to the *Hispaniola*. Ben Gunn was on deck alone. Long John Silver, having taken one bag of coins, was gone. Gunn, it seems, had connived in his escape, and he now assured us he had only done so to preserve our lives from the pirate.

The *Hispaniola* eventually reached Bristol. Only five men of those who had sailed returned with her.

As for the portion of treasure we left behind: The bar silver and the arms still lie, for all that I know, where Flint buried them; and certainly they shall lie there for me. Oxen and wain-ropes would not bring me back again to that accursed island. The worst dreams that ever I have are when I hear the surf booming along its coasts, or start upright in bed, with the sharp voice of Captain Flint, the parrot, still ringing in my ears:
"Pieces of eight!" ✳

What do you think?

Reading a book is like taking a magic carpet ride to a new and different world. While Jim Hawkins and his shipmates sailed aboard the *Hispaniola*, you experienced exciting adventures right along with them! Classic stories like this one are fun to read, and also teach us about the world and ourselves. Wouldn't it be fun to share what you've learned with a brother, sister, friend or parent? Find a quiet spot to talk, then use the questions to discuss *Treasure Island* and the valuable lessons it teaches.

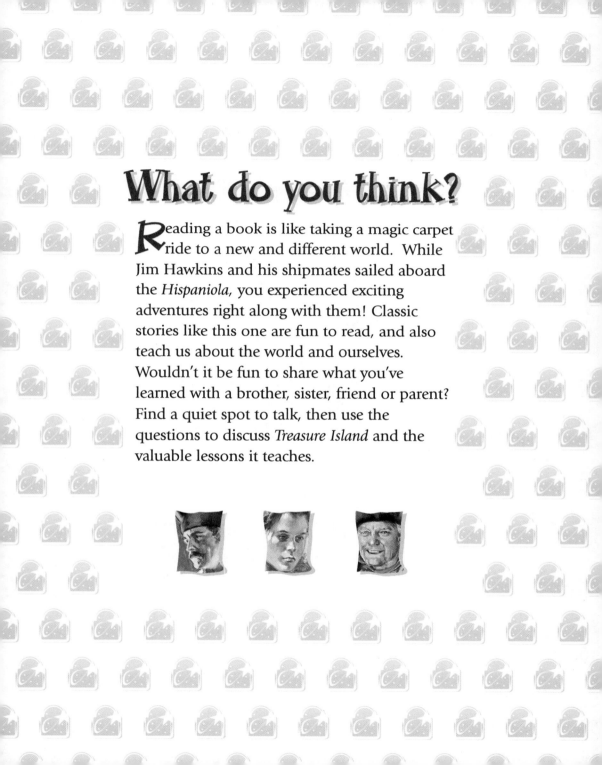

1. *Responsible* people are dependable and keep their word. What promises does Jim make, and keep, in the story?

_____

_____

_____

_____

_____

2. Jim is only a young teen, yet the Squire takes him along on a long and dangerous sea voyage. Why do you think the adults took Jim along on the trip? What qualities did he have that the others respected?

_____

_____

_____

_____

_____

3. Responsible people feel it's their duty to do the right thing. Jim keeps his word to Long John Silver, even though the man is a scoundrel. Why do you think Jim keeps his promise to the pirate?

_____

_____

_____

_____

_____

4. You have things that you are responsible for, such as doing your homework. What other types of jobs are you responsible for at home?

_____

_____

_____

_____

_____